P9-ARF-648

DISCARD

love you

BIG

Vashti Harrison

LB

LITTLE, BROWN AND COMPANY

NEW YORK • BOSTON

ONCE there was a girl

with a big laugh and a big heart

and very big dreams.

R0467513123

She learned her *ABC*s and 123s.

She always said *please* and *thank you*

and even put away all her toys.

At dinner she ate all her food.

"What a big girl you are!" the adults would say.

And it was good.

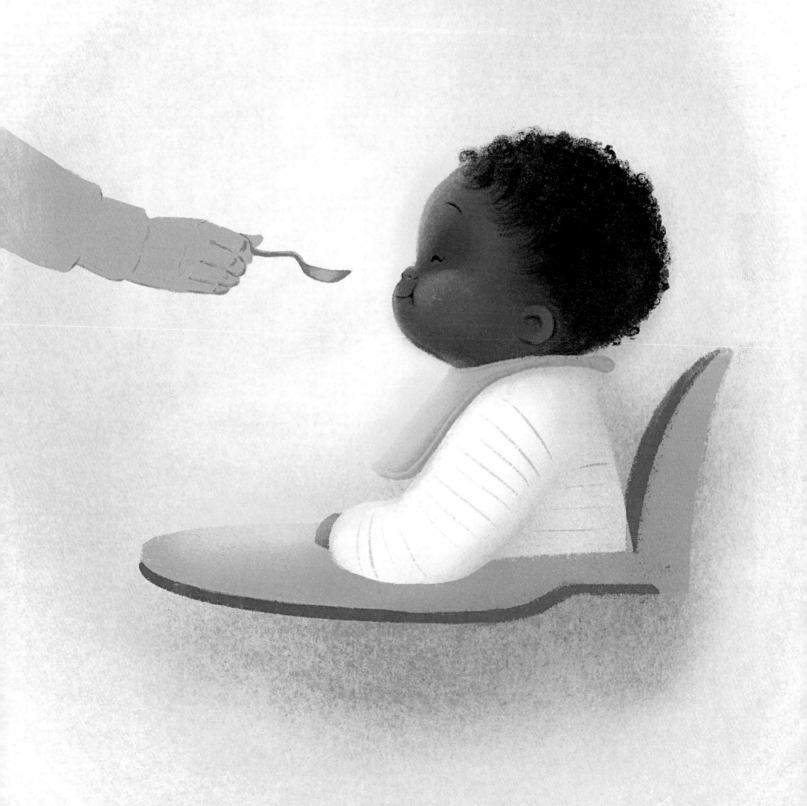

She grew and learned and laughed and dreamed

and grew and grew and grew.

smart

creative

graceful nimble

And it was good . . .

until it wasn't.

One day something big happened.

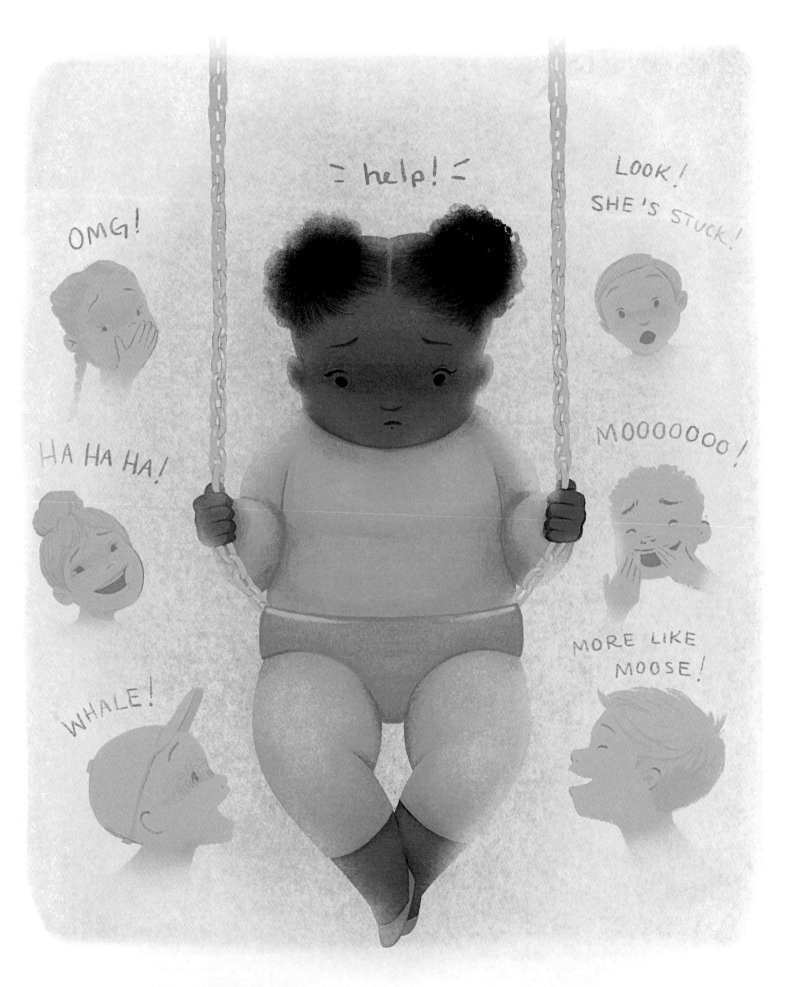

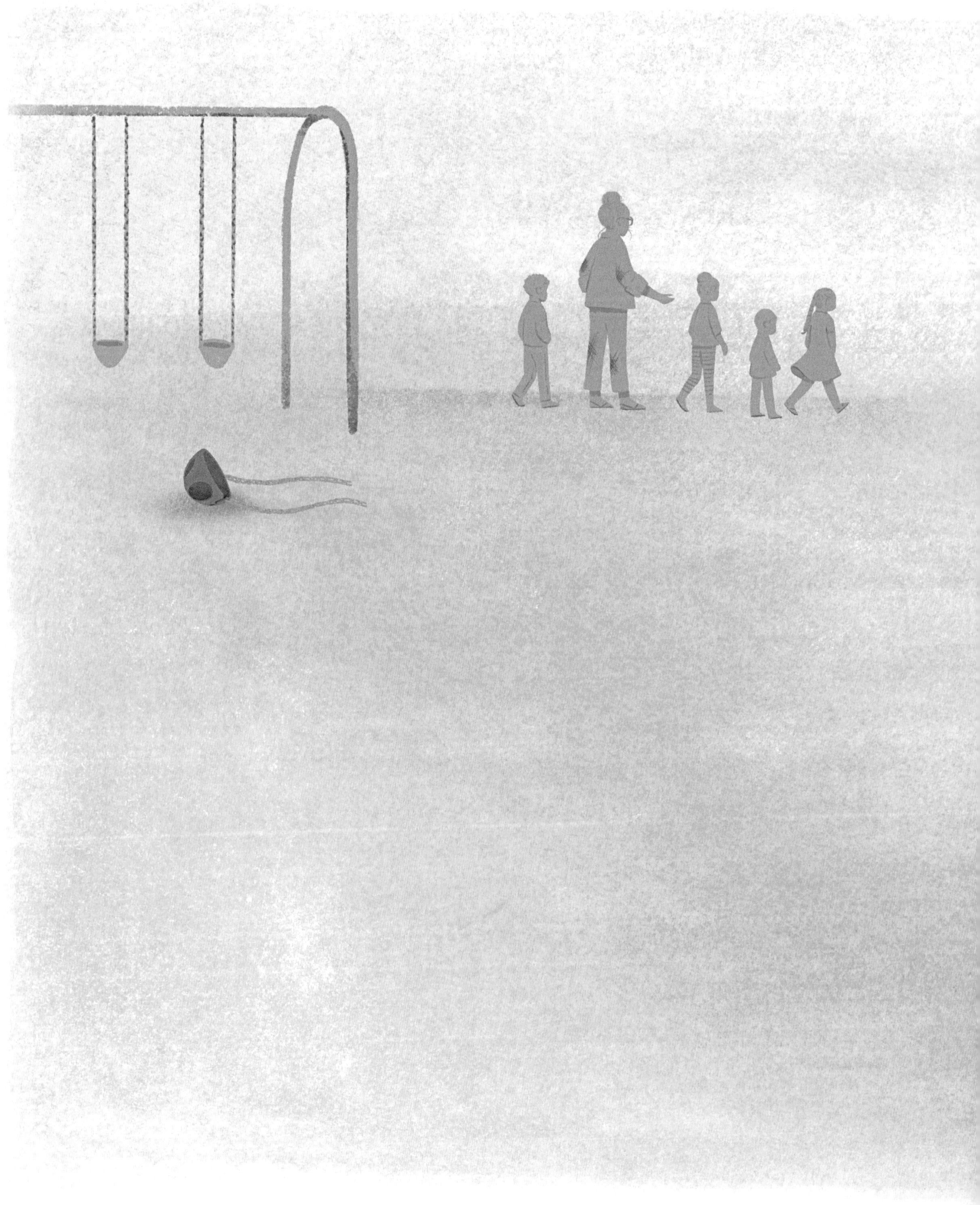

It made her feel small.

The words stung

and were hard to shake off.

She began to feel

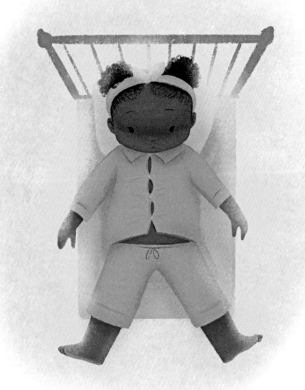

not herself

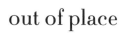
out of place

exposed

judged

yet invisible.

Everyone had advice,

but that kind of hurt, too.

The flower costume won't fit!

You're just too

Where are you going?

What did I say?

big!

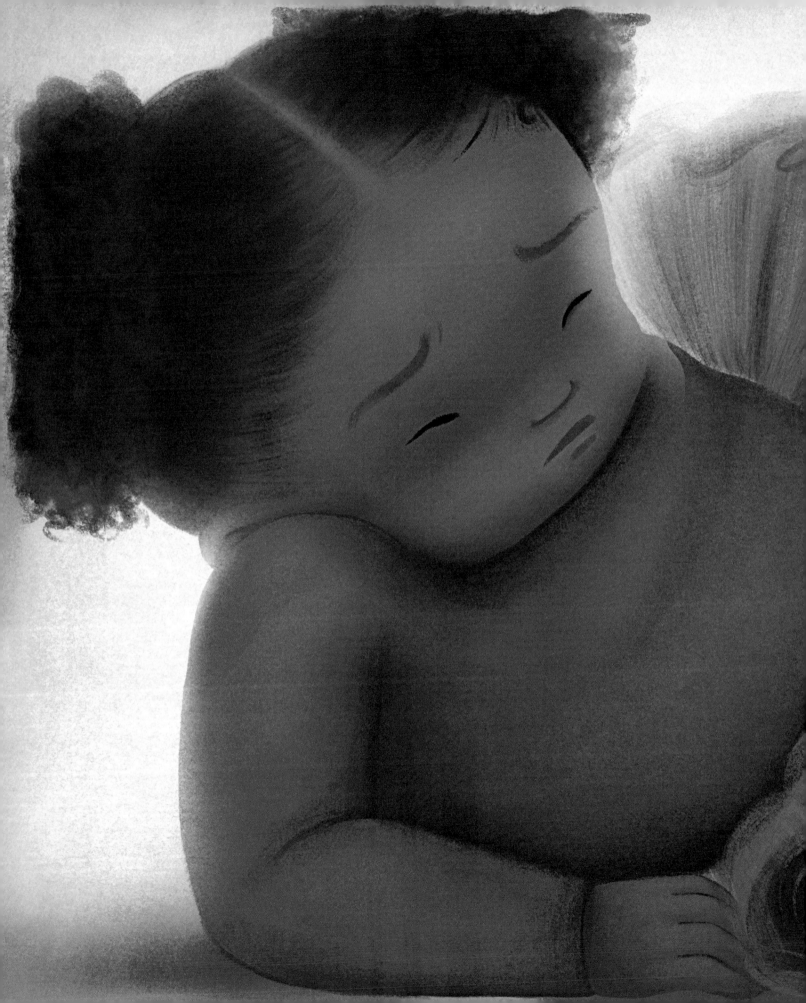

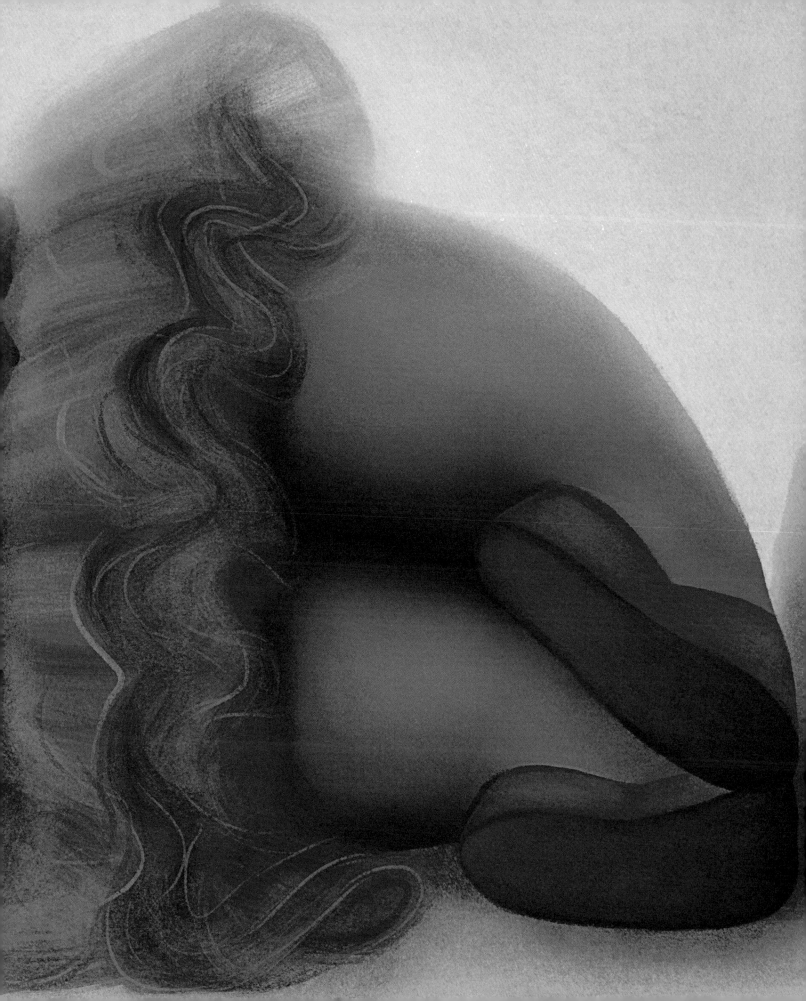

One day she finally let it all out . . .

and started to see

things more clearly.

and was able to see a way out.

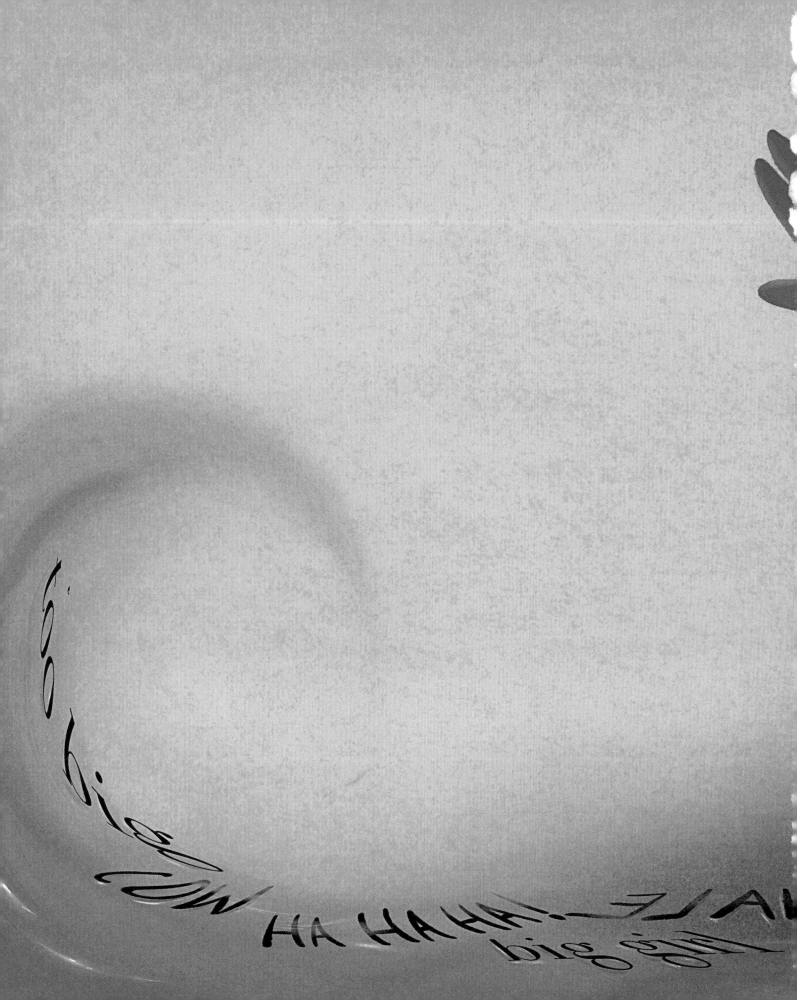

She decided to make

more space for herself . . .

Not everyone understood or even listened.

Some tried . . .

but they still couldn't see

No thank you.
I like the way I am.

that she was just a girl.

imaginative

compassionate

gentle

And she was good.

smart

funny

sweet

AUTHOR'S NOTE

In childhood, big is good. Big is impressive, aspirational. But somewhere along the way, the world begins to tell us something different: That big is bad. That being big is undesirable.

I was never a dancer, but I did get stuck in a swing when I was younger. Some of the older kids and I were playing on the baby swings and I couldn't get out. I was the only one to get into trouble. My size indicated to adults that I was big enough to know better, even though I was still just a kid. I learned that day that my body did not fit. It did not belong. And adults no longer saw me as a little girl who could make innocent mistakes.

While my experience was far less overt than the one in this book, the thoughts and words at work are the same. A child sits in the crosshairs of adultification bias and anti-fat bias. She is subjected to judgments and prejudices that are harmful and have lasting effects. Still, she finds enough self-love to return the words that were unkind and unhelpful. I hope she will stand as a guide to all who need to see her journey, especially those of us who are Black girls in big bodies.

I remember thinking I couldn't wear pink, that it was too bright a color and might make me stand out. From an early age I'd developed insecurities that told me it was safer to shrink into the background and try not to call attention to myself. I chose the color palette for this book to reject that old thinking. In color psychology pink is associated with gentle love, tenderness, and nurturing. Pink flowers symbolize innocence, joy, playfulness, and happiness. These are all things this girl deserves. Her body is not a problem that needs fixing, and neither did mine that day on the playground. What needs fixing are the implicit biases we all hold. I wish I could give the girl a hug—the part of her that is me and the part of her that might be you—and tell her that she is deserving of all the care and joy in the world, no matter what.

ABOUT THIS BOOK

The illustrations for this book were done in Procreate and chalk pastel. This book was edited by Farrin Jacobs, art directed by David Caplan, and designed by Prashansa Thapa. The production was supervised by Nyamekye Waliyaya, and the production editor was Jen Graham. The text was set in Didot LP, and the display type was hand lettered.

Copyright © 2023 by Vashti Harrison • Cover illustration copyright © 2023 by Vashti Harrison • Cover design by Prashansa Thapa • Cover copyright © 2023 by Hachette Book Group, Inc. • Hachette Book Group supports the right to free expression and the value of copyright. The purpose of copyright is to encourage writers and artists to produce the creative works that enrich our culture. • The scanning, uploading, and distribution of this book without permission is a theft of the author's intellectual property. If you would like permission to use material from the book (other than for review purposes), please contact permissions@hbgusa.com. Thank you for your support of the author's rights. • Little, Brown and Company • Hachette Book Group • 1290 Avenue of the Americas, New York, NY 10104 • Visit us at LBYR.com • First Edition: May 2023 • Little, Brown and Company is a division of Hachette Book Group, Inc. • The Little, Brown name and logo are trademarks of Hachette Book Group, Inc • The publisher is not responsible for websites (or their content) that are not owned by the publisher. • Library of Congress Cataloging-in-Publication Data • Names: Harrison, Vashti, author, illustrator. • Title: Big / Vashti Harrison. • Description: First edition. | New York : Little, Brown and Company, 2023. | Audience: Ages 4–8. | Summary: Praised for acting like a big girl when she is small, as a young girl grows, "big" becomes a word of criticism, until the girl realizes that she is fine just the way she is. • Identifiers: LCCN 2021034390 | ISBN 9780316353229 (hardcover) • Subjects: LCSH: Physical-appearance-based bias—Juvenile fiction. | Identity (Psychology)—Juvenile fiction. | Self-acceptance—Juvenile fiction. | CYAC: Growth—Fiction. | Self-acceptance—Fiction. • Classification: LCC PZ7.1.H37553 Bi 2022 | DDC [E]—dc23 • LC record available at https://lccn.loc.gov/2021034390 • ISBN 978-0-316-35322-9 • PRINTED IN CHINA • APS • 10 9 8 7 6 5 4 3 2